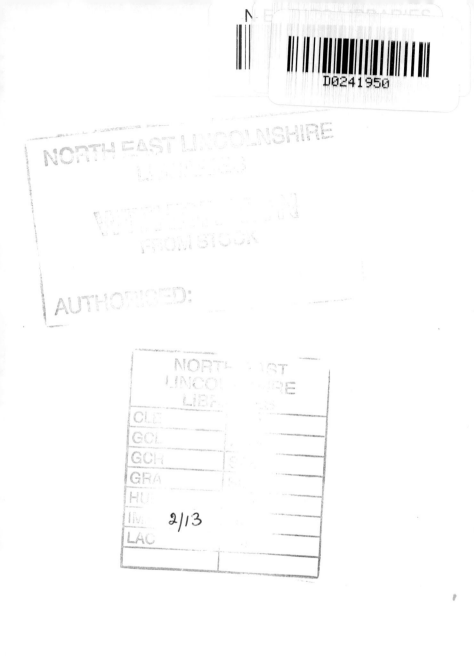

The Circus Mice

Level 4E

Written by Isabel Crawford
Illustrated by Kimberley Scott

What is synthetic phonics?

Synthetic phonics teaches children to recognise the sounds of letters and to blend (synthesise) them together to make whole words.

Understanding sound/letter relationships gives children the confidence and ability to read unfamiliar words, without having to rely on memory or guesswork; this helps them to progress towards independent reading.

Did you know? Spoken English uses more than 40 speech sounds. Each sound is called a *phoneme*. Some phonemes relate to a single letter (d-o-g) and others to combinations of letters (sh-ar-p). When a phoneme is written down it is called a *grapheme*. Teaching these sounds, matching them to their written form and sounding out words for reading is the basis of synthetic phonics.

Consultant

I love reading phonics has been created in consultation with language expert Abigail Steel. She has a background in teaching and teacher training and is a respected expert in the field of synthetic phonics. Abigail Steel is a regular contributor to educational publications. Her international education consultancy supports parents and teachers in the promotion of literacy skills.

Reading tips

This book focuses on the igh sound, made with the letter formation i-e, as in kite.

Tricky words in this book

Any words in bold may have unusual spellings or are new and have not yet been introduced.

Tricky words in this book:

circus mice one two paws ice while four what ready guess believe

Extra ways to have fun with this book

After the reader has read the story, ask them questions about what they have just read:

What skill did mouse number one have?

Which mouse is your favourite?

Roll up! Roll up! Welcome to the Fine Time Circus! We hope you'll have a mighty fine time!

A pronunciation guide

This grid contains the sounds used in the stories in levels 4, 5 and 6 and a guide on how to say them. /a/ represents the sounds made, rather than the letters in a word.

/ai/ as in game	/ai/ as in play/they	/ee/ as in leaf/these	/ee/ as in he
/igh/ as in kite/light	/igh/ as in find/sky	/oa/ as in home	/oa/ as in snow
/oa/ as in cold	/y+oo/ as in cube/music/new	long /oo/ as in flute/crew/blue	/oi/ as in boy
/er/ as in bird/hurt	/or/ as in snore/oar/door	/or/ as in dawn/sauce/walk	/e/ as in head
/e/ as in said/any	/ou/ as in cow	/u/ as in touch	/air/ as in hare/bear/there
/eer/ as in deer/here/cashier	/t/ as in tripped/skipped	/d/ as in rained	/j/ as in gent/gin/gym
/j/ as in barge/hedge	/s/ as in cent/circus/cyst	/s/ as in prince	/s/ as in house
/ch/ as in itch/catch	/w/ as in white	/h/ as in who	/r/ as in write/rhino

Sounds this story focuses on are highlighted in the grid.

/**f**/ as in phone	/**f**/ as in rough	/**ul**/ as in pencil/ hospital	/**z**/ as in fries/ cheese/breeze
/**n**/ as in knot/ gnome/engine	/**m**/ as in welcome /thumb/column	/**g**/ as in guitar/ghost	/**zh**/ as in vision/beige
/**k**/ as in chord	/**k**/ as in plaque/ bouquet	/**nk**/ as in uncle	/**ks**/ as in box/books/ ducks/cakes
/**a**/ and /**o**/ as in hat/what	/**e**/ and /**ee**/ as in bed/he	/**i**/ and /**igh**/ as in fin/find	/**o**/ and /**oa**/ as in hot/cold
/**u**/ and short /**oo**/ as in but/put	/**ee**/, /**e**/ and /**ai**/ as in eat/ bread/break	/**igh**/, /**ee**/ and /**e**/ as in tie/field/friend	/**ou**/ and /**oa**/ as in cow/blow
/**ou**/, /**oa**/ and /**oo**/ as in out/ shoulder/could	/**i**/ and /**ai**/ as in money/they	/**c**/ and /**s**/ as in cat/cent	/**y**/, /**igh**/ and /**i**/ as in yes/sky/myth
/**g**/ and /**j**/ as in got/giant	/**ch**/, /**c**/ and /**sh**/ as in chin/ school/chef	/**er**/, /**air**/ and /**eer**/ as in earth/bear/ears	/**u**/, /**ou**/ and /**oa**/ as in plough/dough

Be careful not to add an 'uh' sound to 's', 't', 'p', 'c', 'h', 'r', 'm', 'd', 'g', 'l', 'f' and 'b'. For example, say 'fff' not 'fuh' and 'sss' not 'suh'.

Have you ever been to
the Fine Time **Circus**?
They have five spectacular
performing **mice**.
And each of them has a
different skill, each more
spectacular than the last...

Number **one** can ride a bike
and fly a kite.

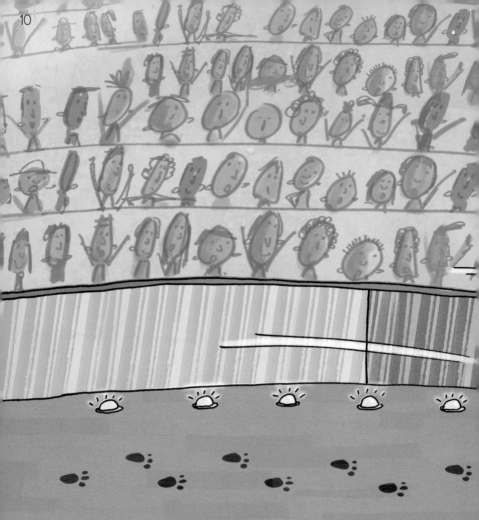

Number **two** can run a mile
on his front **paws**.

Number three can skate on **ice** **while** dining on pineapple.

Number **four** can sky dive and juggle fire.

"But **what** can number five do?"
I hear you ask.

Are you **ready** for it?
Can you **guess**?

Number five can
ride a bike,
fly a kite,
run a mile,
skate on ice,
dine on pineapple,
sky dive and juggle fire...
at the same time!

If you don't **believe** me then you
must go to the Fine Time Circus
to see the five performing mice
for yourself.

OVER **48** TITLES IN SIX LEVELS
Abigail Steel recommends...

Other titles to enjoy from Level 4

I love reading phonics — Monster's **Night**
978-1-84898-583-4

I love reading phonics — **Jemima the Spy**
978-1-84898-584-1

I love reading phonics — **The Mummy Code**
978-1-84898-585-8

Some titles from Level 5

I love reading phonics — **The Gigantic Bear**
978-1-84898-586-5

I love reading phonics — **Celebrity Celia**
978-1-84898-587-2

I love reading phonics — **The Cemetery Dance**
978-1-84898-588-9

Some titles from Level 6

I love reading phonics — **Hugh is New**
978-1-84898-590-2

I love reading phonics — **Clumsy Eagle**
978-1-84898-591-9

I love reading phonics — **Bad Zombie Movie**
978-1-84898-592-6

An Hachette UK Company
www.hachette.co.uk

Copyright © Octopus Publishing Group Ltd 2012
First published in Great Britain in 2012 by TickTock, an imprint of Octopus Publishing Group Ltd,
Endeavour House, 189 Shaftesbury Avenue, London WC2H 8JY.
www.octopusbooks.co.uk

ISBN 978 1 84898 582 7

Printed and bound in China
10 9 8 7 6 5 4 3 2 1